To my son Freddie and all the children who have ever been afraid, but were willing to put their faith in God to overcome their fears.

-Tasha Fuller

2 Timothy 1:7 New King James Version
For God has not given us a spirit of fear,
but of power and of love and of a sound mind.

To AJ, whose life exemplifies God's limitless love and compassion.

-Apryl Boersma

ISBN   979-8-4716233-3-0

Library of Congress Control Number: 2021902342

www.TashasBooks.com

First Edition

Daddy, I'm Scared!

Written by Tasha Fuller
Illustrated by Apryl G. Boersma

Published by Your Go2 Girls, Inc.

ISBN 979-8-4716233-3-0

WWW.TASHASBOOKS.COM

I take my bath,

I say my prayers,

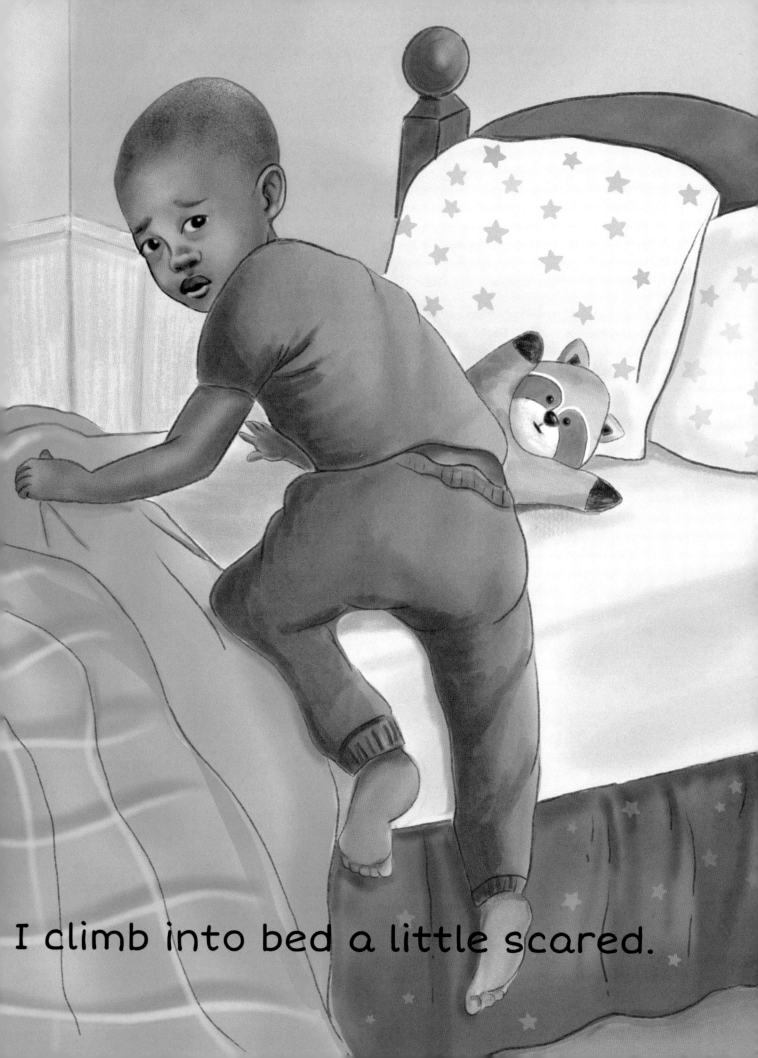

I climb into bed a little scared.

I kiss my dad and say goodnight,
He hugs me close and says sleep tight.

The lights go down throughout the hall.
I see a scary monster on the wall.

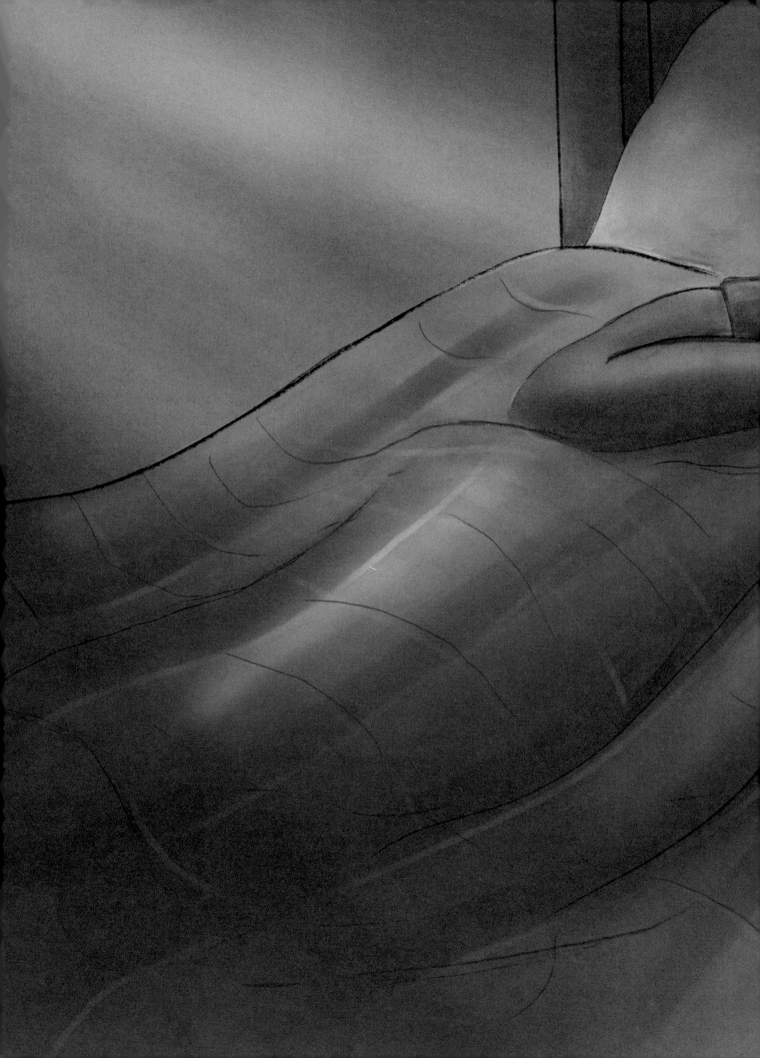

I hear a noise
I shake in my bed,

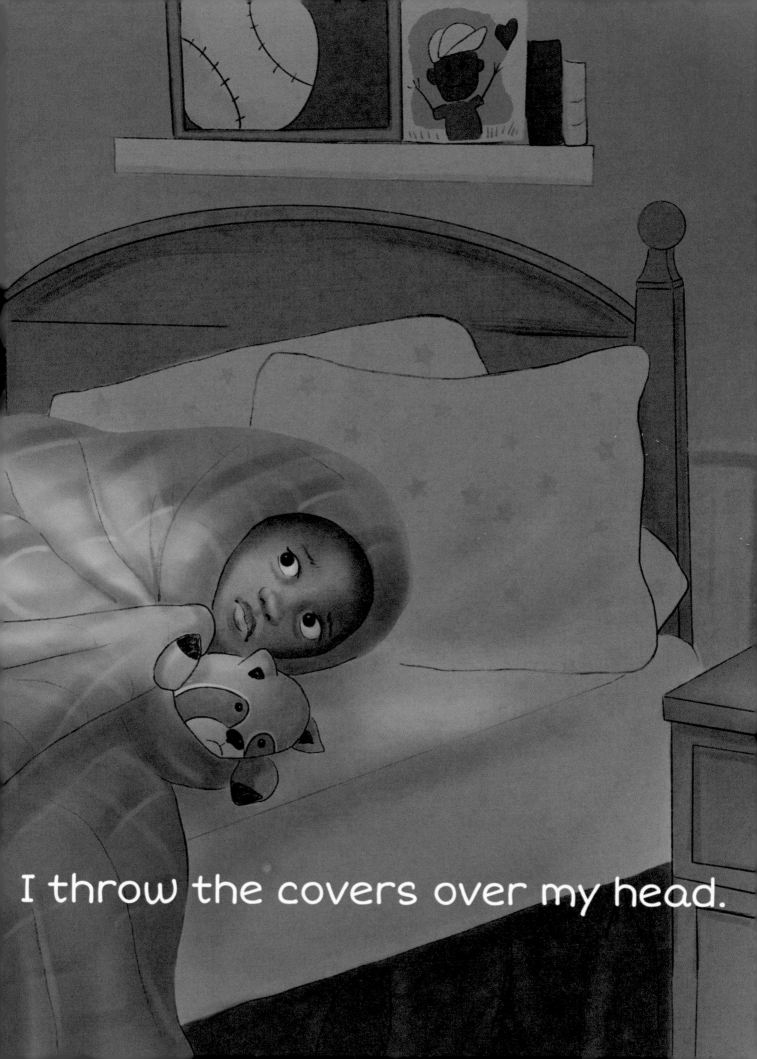

I throw the covers over my head.

The window creaks,
I jump from the sound,

Off I go running until daddy is found.

He lays in bed still a slumber.
He's not scared.
So, I stop and wonder.

But, I wake him anyway
because I am scared.

He looks under the bed
He checks the stairs
to assure me
there are no monsters here.

He gave me a hug,
He said sleep tight.
He said God will watch us
through the night.

Then we got on our knees
and said a quick prayer.

"God please take away this
spirit of fear.
Keep and protect me
I pray to the Lord.
Encamp your angels around
our door."

So, back in my bed
to sleep through the night,

I closed my eyes,
believing that everything
will be alright.

Other Titles You May Enjoy

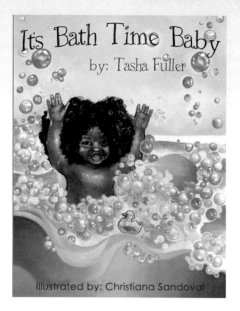

WWW.TASHASBOOKS.com

I love God because:

_____
_____
_____
_____

I ask God's forgiveness for:

_____
_____
_____
_____

I thank God for my blessings:

_____
_____
_____
_____

My prayers for myself and others:

_____
_____
_____
_____
_____
_____

Amen

For more information regarding author visits, school fundraisers or bulk orders, please email

Akcfuller@gmail.com

Tasha Fuller
Author

Tasha is a Stay at Home Mother of four, Wife, Author, Self Publishing Coach and consummate creator. Bitten by the writing bug in 2013 with the publication of her first book, ***"It's Bath Time Baby"***, Tasha has gone on to publish five other titles, "***Little Freddie's in a Zone", "Mommy, I Want to Dance", "Mommy, I Want to be a Princess***", her chapter book ***"Making the Squad"*** and her latest release, ***"Daddy, I'm Scared!"***

As an author Tasha has been blessed with some amazing opportunities. Her book entitled, ***"It's Bath Time Baby"***, was selected to be apart of the early childhood development curriculum for the State of Maryland, the same title was also selected to be apart of the New York City PBS affiliate WNET/Thirteen "Let's Learn", a virtual program that helps children ages 3-8 with at-home learning. In addition, Tasha works with the City of Milwaukee's Office of Early Childhood Initiatives, and has been a featured author with Richmond City Public Schools, DC Public Schools, Prince William County Public Schools, as well as numerous other school systems and organizations.

Tasha's journey as an author and publisher gives her an opportunity to share her gifts and successes while inspiring authors through the process, as well as giving opportunities to aspiring illustrators.

Apryl Greene Boersma
Illustrator

Apryl is a faithful wife, loving mother of 3, and adoring daughter. Her passion for art started at the tender age of 5 under her mother's Ernestine dining room table. Her family always encouraged her interest in art and her skillful father, Freddie, even created special tools for her to use. As a child she spent hours collaborating with her brother, Lee, on his comic strips, and in high school one of her sculptures was chosen for a year-long tour of China.

When she attended college she was exposed to various art mediums, her favorite being ceramics. However, after taking a course in human anatomy to help with her drawing skills, she was inspired to become a registered nurse. After a career in the nursing field Apryl returned to her passion and started teaching.

She desires to create a positive art experience by building her students' confidence as they develop their skills. Apryl taught elementary and high school art for 6 years before she started teaching art classes to disabled adults. "Daddy, I'm Scared!", is Apryl's first book.

Apryl resides in Northern Virginia with her husband, Dan, her children, AJ, Brianna, Olivia and her mother, Ernestine.   Romans 11:36

Made in the USA
Middletown, DE
28 August 2022

72236938R00022